BIONICLE

JOURNEY OF TAKANUVA

BY GREG FARSHTEY

ILLUSTRATED BY
JEREMY BRAZEAL

SCHOLASTIC INC.

NEW YORK   TORONTO   LONDON   AUCKLAND   SYDNEY

MEXICO CITY   NEW DELHI   HONG KONG   BUENOS AIRES

ISBN–10: 0-545-08214-5
ISBN–13: 978-0-545-08214-3

LEGO, the LEGO logo and BIONICLE are trademarks of the LEGO Group and used here by special permission. © 2008 The LEGO Group.

12 11 10 9 8 7 6 5 4 3   9 10/0

Book designed by Cheung Tai and Henry Ng
Printed in the U.S.A.
First printing, September 2008

Takanuva was a special kind of hero. He was a Toa. He controlled the power of light and wore a mask called the Avohkii, or Mask of Light. He had not been a Toa for long, but he had already had many adventures. He thought he knew everything there was to know about being a hero.

Today, he was on a new mission. He had to find six other Toa who were in a faraway place called Karda Nui. Takanuva had important news to tell them and had to reach them as fast as he could. To do this, he had to travel between dimensions.

But things did not go as planned. Takanuva fell through a hole in space and landed hard on the ground of a strange world. He got up and looked around. He was in the center of a forest. But it was a very strange forest. All the trees were black and twisted, and the grass was dying. A cold wind blew and made him shiver.

A voice spoke behind him. "A visitor!"

Takanuva turned to see a mask floating in midair. The voice was coming from the mask, but that made no sense. Masks couldn't talk, they were just . . . masks.

"Who are you?" asked the mask.

"I'm a Toa," said Takanuva. "That's a hero. Can you show me the way out? I have a mission I must carry out."

The mask smiled, which was a very strange sight. "Oh, if you are a hero, you are just what we need. Help us, and perhaps we can help you. There is a village on the other side of that hill that is in terrible trouble. You see, there is a —"

"All right," Takanuva interrupted. "I'll go and take care of the problem. Then you can help me get on my way."

The mask looked like it was going to say something, but then just smiled instead. "All right. Good luck to you, Toa hero!"

Takanuva ran to the top of the hill. He stopped and stared. The "village" was more like a gigantic city, bigger than anything he had ever seen. Towers of silver reached up to the sky, surrounded by buildings made of gleaming crystal. It was beautiful.

It was easy to see what trouble the mask had been talking about. The city was full of small beings wearing black and purple armor. They were fighting a monster that was attacking their city. The monster was at least twenty feet high, with pointed ears, huge claws, and a a mouth full of sharp teeth. The villagers were fighting hard, but Takanuva was sure they would lose.

He fired a burst of light from his power lance, temporarily blinding the monster. "Get back!" Takanuva yelled to the small beings. "I'll handle this!" The monster growled. For a moment, Takanuva thought he heard the beast speak, but decided he must be mistaken.

The monster tried to hit Takanuva, but the Toa of Light was too fast for him. A few more bolts of light from the Toa's lance, and the beast began to stagger. It growled again, more loudly. This time, Takanuva was sure he heard the monster saying, "Wait! Stop! You're wrong!"

It must be trying to trick me, Takanuva said to himself.
I know an evil monster when I see one.

Takanuva hurled one more light blast from his lance
and this one hit the monster. It roared in pain and ran
off into the woods. Takanuva expected to hear cheering
from the villagers . Instead, all he heard was laughter.
Then they slammed and barred the gates so he could
not get into the city.

The Toa of Light was puzzled, confused, and a little hurt. He had risked his life to save them and they hadn't even said thank you! He knocked on the gates, but no one answered.

He found the floating mask again. "I did it," said Takanuva. "I defeated the big monster and saved the city."

"You defeated the big monster? Oh, no," said the mask. "What have you done?"

"What's the matter?" asked Takanuva.

"That 'monster' was the last of the beings that lived in that city," the mask explained.

"The little armored ones were invaders who took it away from him. They were the trouble. I started to tell you, but you were in too much of a hurry to listen."

"But he had sharp teeth and claws," protested Takanuva. "And he was so big, and they were so little, so I thought . . ."

"Good does not always come in little packages, or evil in big ones," said the mask. "My giant friend is gentle and kind, and uses his teeth and claws only to defend himself. I'm sure he would have told you that if he'd had the chance."

"He tried," said Takanuva, turning away. "I didn't listen." The next moment, the Toa of Light was running away.

"Where are you going?" asked the mask.

"To correct a mistake," answered Takanuva.

It took a while to find the wounded beast, and longer still to convince him that Takanuva meant no harm. The mask had been right.

The beast didn't want to harm the invaders, just get them out of his city. Takanuva thought he had an idea that would do just that.

An hour later, the Toa stood on the top of a big hill about half a mile from the city gates. He lifted his lance and hurled light into the sky. His powers created the most amazing fireworks show anyone had ever seen!

One by one, the small invaders came out of the city to watch the bursts of light in the sky. Soon, there was a whole crowd of them, all looking up in wonder.

They were so caught up in the light show that none of them noticed the beast emerging from a tunnel into the center of the city. It had taken him a long time to dig his way home, but now he was back. Striding to the huge gates, the beast slammed them shut, trapping the invaders outside the walls of the city.

Takanuva smiled. Since he had arrived here, he had been making mistakes because he judged others by how they looked. Now the invaders had done the same thing, by thinking the fireworks were just fireworks. As a result, they had lost the city they had stolen and would never get it back.

When he returned to the floating mask, it seemed pleased with him. "All beings make mistakes, at some time," said the mask. "But part of being a hero is admitting you were wrong and fixing them. You have done that well."

A hole appeared in space next to the mask. "Is this my way out of here?" asked Takanuva. "I need to get to my friends before it's too late!"

"It is the way you must travel," said the mask. "But beware — you may find that not everything is what it seems on your way. Remember, good and evil can be found in the deeds of others, not in their appearance."

"I'll remember," said Takanuva. "And . . . thank you."
With that, the Toa of Light dove through the hole and into the space between dimensions. Where his journey would take him, he didn't know — but he did know that he was much wiser now than when it began.